Octopus Soup

Mercer Mayer

Marshall Cavendish Children

Marshall Cavendish Corporation, 99 White Plains Road, Tarrytown, NY 10591

www.marshallcavendish.us/kids

Library of Congress Cataloging-in-Publication Data

Mayer, Mercer, 1943-

Octopus soup / by Mercer Mayer. — 1st ed.

p. cm.

Summary: An octopus struggles with misadventure when he leaves home but is
relieved to know how and where to find a safe haven.

ISBN 978-0-7614-5812-8

[1. Octopuses—Fiction. 2. Stories without words.] 1. Title.

PZ7.M462Oc 2011

2010021232

The illustrations are rendered in Photoshop.

Book design by Anahid Hamparian

Editor: Margery Cuyler

Printed in China (E)
First edition
1 3 5 6 4 2

To Arden, Benjamin, and Zebulon,
whose budding art careers make
me a proud dad

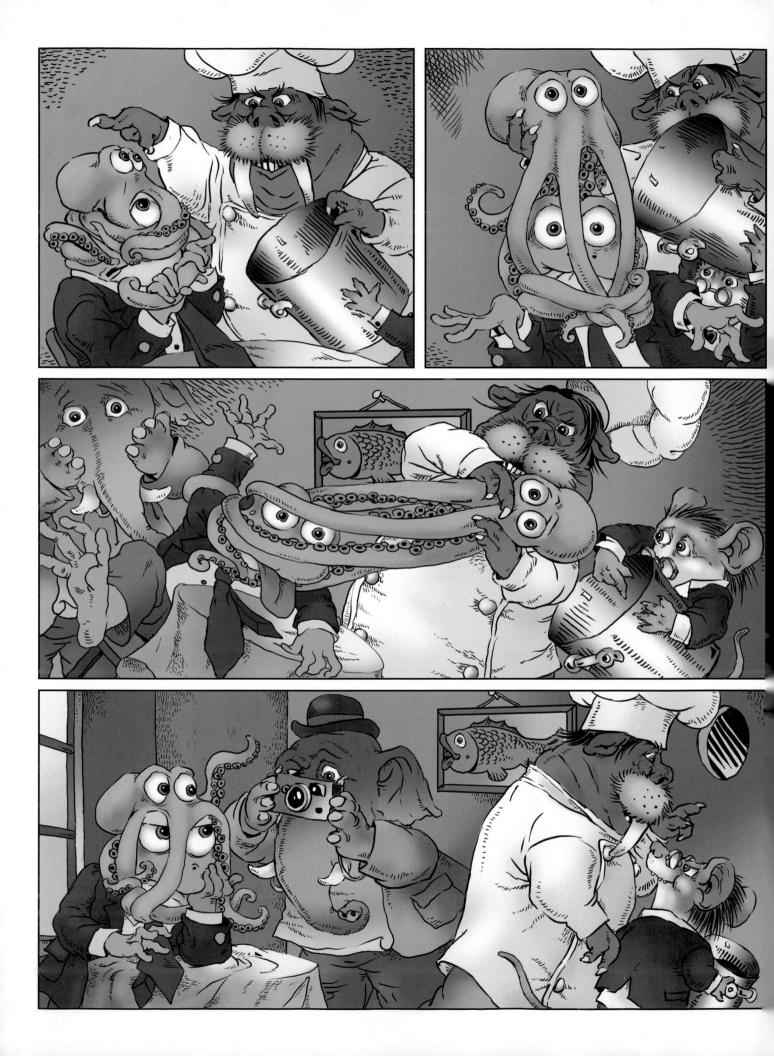

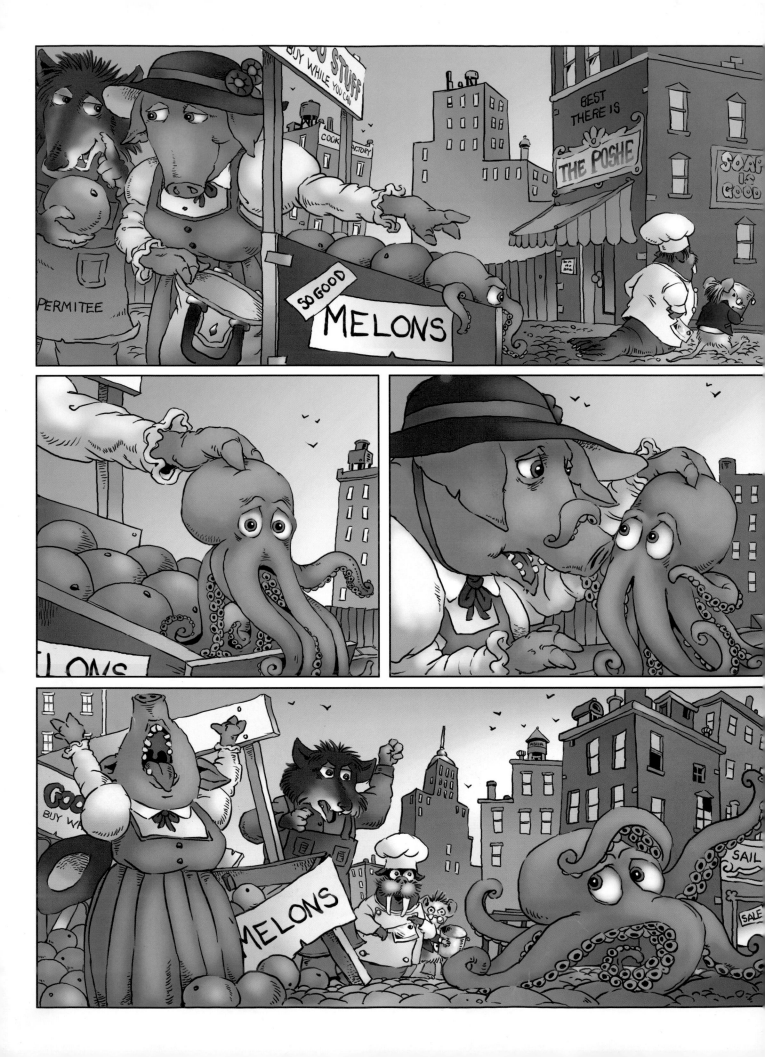

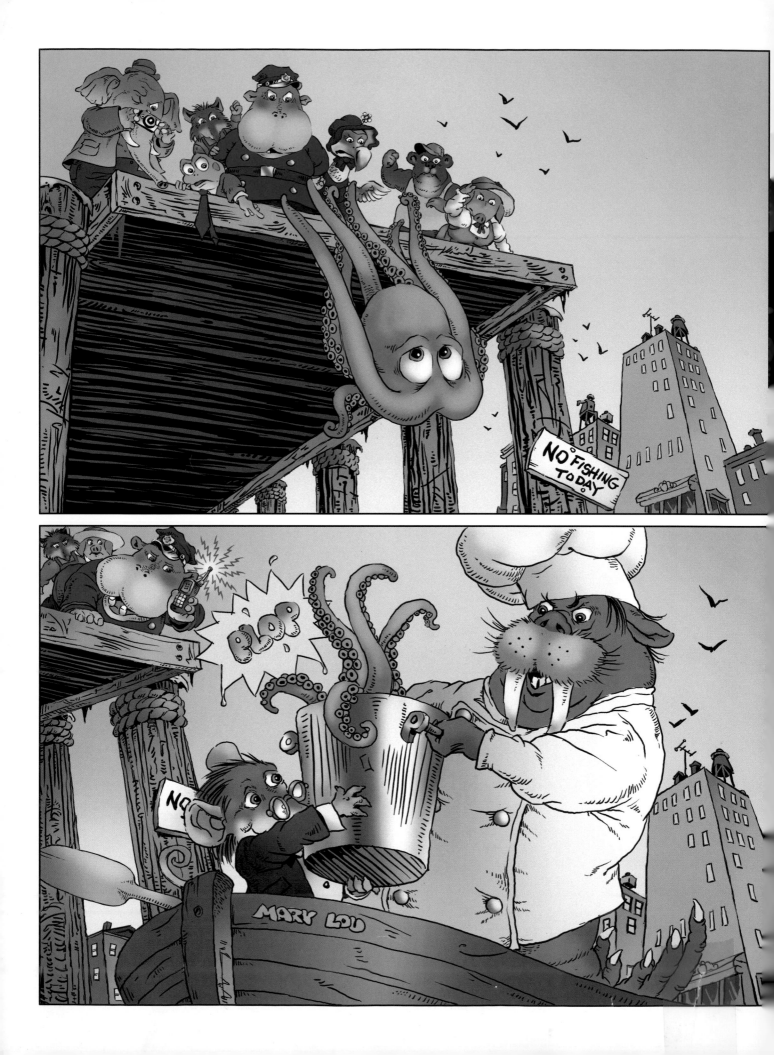

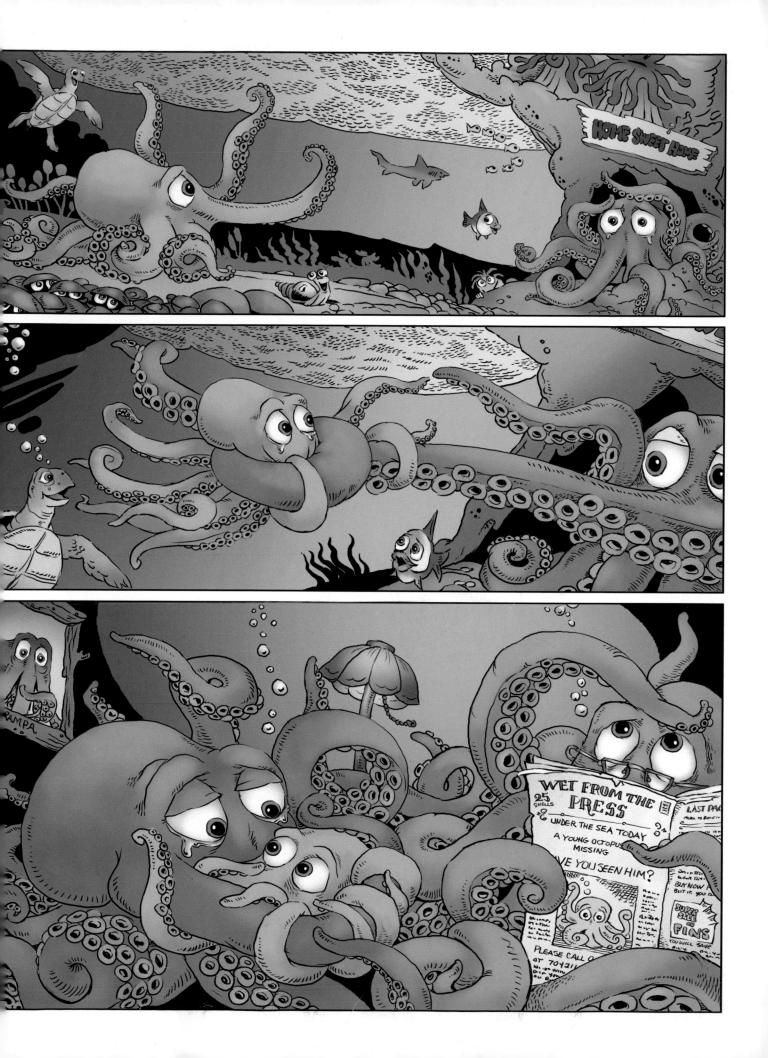